George's Antlers

Bruno St-Aubin

Scholastic Canada Ltd.
Toronto New York London Auckland Sydney
Mexico City New Delhi Hong Kong Buenos Aires

My thanks to Jean Paquin for his wonderful books on birds.

My respects to the enormous talent of Robert Bateman. Thank you!

The illustrations for this book were created in watercolour on Arches paper.

The type was set in 19.5 point Langer.

Scholastic Canada Ltd.
604 King Street West, Toronto, Ontario M5V 1E1, Canada

Scholastic Inc.
557 Broadway, New York, NY 10012, USA

Scholastic Australia Pty Limited
PO Box 579, Gosford, NSW 2250, Australia

Scholastic New Zealand Limited
Private Bag 94407, Botany, Manukau 2163, New Zealand

Scholastic Children's Books
Euston House, 24 Eversholt Street, London NW1 1DB, UK

Library and Archives Canada Cataloguing in Publication
[St-Aubin, Bruno
[Panache du grand Georges. English]
George's antlers / written and illustrated by Bruno St-Aubin ; translated by Petra Johannson.

Translation of: Le panache du grand Georges.

1. Moose--Juvenile fiction. 2. Birds--Juvenile fiction. I. Johannson, Petra
II. Title: Panache du grand Georges.

PS8587.A255P3413 2010   jC843'.54   C2009-906322-0

6 5 4 3 2 1   Printed in Canada 119   10 11 12 13 14

Mixed Sources
Product group from well-managed
forests and other controlled sources
www.fsc.org Cert no. SGS-COC-003098
© 1996 Forest Stewardship Council
FSC

For Simone and Giuseppe

Near the edge of a quiet lake surrounded by trees, George browsed peacefully on his lunch.

All of a sudden he heard a crackling sound.

Then he smelled smoke.

A forest fire! George was terrified of fire.
As his friends flew off through the smoke,
he galloped away as fast as he could.

He ran and ran, and finally stopped for breath in a wide, swampy meadow. He was safe at last, and very relieved that he hadn't been barbecued. But, in his mad dash, he had become totally lost.

His head was spinning, and his heart was racing as he thought of his friends. They were so small and helpless!

"Where are they? I hope nothing has happened to them, especially little Ruby. Oh, this is awful!" George moaned.

In the distance, he saw Bonnie and Rufus struggling to drag their nest.

"George! George! We need your help!" they cried.

"I'm so glad to see you! Hang on to my antlers."

14

Gratefully, Bonnie and Rufus
nudged their nest into place.
What a good friend George was!

But he was still worried about Ruby. She was so tiny. "Oh, this is awful . . ."

"George! George! I need your help!" It was Otis. "There's not one branch left to perch on. I'm so exhausted, flapping around with nowhere to land," he wheezed.

"Otis! I'm so glad to see you!" cried George, offering his antlers.

Very pleased, Otis settled in. George was thrilled to have found him, but he was still worried about Ruby. She was so little.

"Oh, this is awful . . ."

"George! George! I need your help. The trees have all burned down, and I've lost too many feathers to fly," whimpered Suzy.

"Suzy! I'm so glad to see you! Make yourself at home here," said George, leaning forward.

Relieved, Suzy perched on his antlers. George was happy to have found her, but he was still worried about little Ruby.

"George! George! We need your help," begged Big Beak and Jay-Jay, their wings blackened by smoke.

"Big Beak! Jay-Jay! I'm so glad to see you!" cried George.

Safe and sound in his antlers, the two friends told jokes while they preened their feathers. George chuckled a little, but as soon as he thought of Ruby, his heart sank.

"Oh, this is awful . . ."

"George! George! We need your help," pleaded Marsha and Mask, Hammer and Hummer, Captain, Twitter, Cedric and the rest of the gang.

"Oh, I'm so glad to see you all again!" said George, inviting all of them to stay — even though the load was getting heavier and heavier.

George's friends had never imagined such a
wonderful place to live. Every night, they had
a party . . .

...and every morning, they sang.

In George's antlers, they were completely safe. The foxes and the weasels couldn't touch them.

But Ruby was still missing. And George was still worried about his best friend.

And then . . . she arrived! George was
exhausted, but he lifted his heavy head
to welcome his dearest friend. She landed
gently on the end of his great nose, as she
always did, and . . .

KABOOM! A thunderous noise rumbled across the meadow. Poor George, at the end of his strength, had crashed to the ground.

His friends were in a terrible flutter, but
they worked hard to help him back to
his feet.

Then they settled him into a beautiful, big nest. "What good friends I have!" he murmured, smiling. "Oh, this is *wonderful!*"